Morcant

Morcant

ASHER ALLEN

Morcant

Copyright © 2023 by Asher Allen

ISBN: 978-1-312-80753-2

Printed in the United States of America.

The life of the flesh is in the blood.

—Leviticus

1

The iron poker punctured my left lung. My girlfriend put such force into the thrust, it would have stabbed clean through to the hardwood floor beneath me if the makeshift spear had only encountered skin and muscle and vital organs. But the tip struck a rib at my back.

My breath left me in a wheezing gasp. The pain was the worst I had felt in decades—perhaps even a century.

Standing over my prone body, my girlfriend tried to wrench the poker free of my chest, undoubtedly to skewer me again. But I caught hold of the metal rod, and no mortal woman would have been able to withdraw it then.

Melanie gave a good hard yank, but then gave up and fled from the room. To get the gun, most likely.

Lying there on the floor of our dining room, I sighed. A very painful action, but I could not help it.

This relationship had been going so well. I had thought it might last at least another few years or so.

I pulled the fire iron from my chest, coughed up blood, then staggered to my feet.

My flesh was already repairing itself.

I stood there, the bloody skewer in my hand. Loath to let good blood go to waste, I licked the poker clean.

It was fortunate Melanie had not gone for the fancy silverware instead of the fire iron. I supposed she did not think of a butter knife as much of a weapon, but even a spoon of real silver would have served her better than any instrument of base metal.

When the first two bullets took me in the gut, I decided I was done with long-term relationships for the foreseeable future. I would take short-term lovers, not live-in girlfriends.

"*Die*, you monster!"

Melanie fired again, and the bullet punched a hole in my right lung.

Always so hot-tempered, that girl.

Those first two bullets clattered to the floor, expelled from my healing body back through the entry wounds. I coughed the third bullet up from my lung.

"Are you sure we can't talk about this, Mel?"

A bullet clipped my ear.

One of my past lovers, circa the late eighteenth century, had actually accepted me for who I was. I did not leave her after the usual decade or so, but remained mostly loyal to her almost until she became an old woman.

She *had* considered herself something of a witch, so maybe that had something to do with it.

I raised my hand, as though I could ward off Mel's next shot, but the bullet punched through my hand and entered my shoulder. Two holes for the price of one.

"Mel, it really wasn't what it looked like."

I assumed she thought I was cheating on her when she came home early and found me with a girl. But it was really all quite innocent. Just drawing a pint or two of blood—and consensually, no less.

Melanie kept firing and screaming.

I thought of killing her, pinning her to the wall with the poker in my hand. But I do not like killing my women if it is not absolutely necessary.

Besides, I could smell the garlic on her breath from where I stood, so I would not even be able to consume her blood if I did end her.

Mel ran out of bullets, and ran upstairs, presumably to retrieve more.

I took the opportunity to make my way posthaste to the garage, where I grabbed my bugout bag, and drove away.

Once outside the city limits, I pulled off on the side of the road. I pried the side panel off my door and took out one of my identity packets. Driver's license, passport, and credit card under the name Saul Stoker.

I also took out a spare set of license plates and swapped them with the existing ones.

From my bag, I fished out hair clippers. I buzzed my hair down to stubble, and regretfully razed my mustache.

I looked at myself in the mirror—it having no silver backing—and nodded to myself.

"Hello, Saul, you handsome devil."

2

"When does your shift end?"

"About an hour from now," the waitress said.

"What are you doing after that?"

"Nothing really."

I smiled. "Would you like to be doing something?"

A few months had passed since I left Melanie, and I now sat talking with this ravishing little blonde at a diner in some tiny Colorado town. Kendra was her name, according to the nametag on her uniform apron. There was no one else in the diner, and the voice of Don Henley serenaded us with "Desperado."

"I have a boyfriend," Kendra said.

"So?"

"You don't see the problem?"

"Does he live with you?"

"No."

"Then what's the problem? Does he control you? Are you a free woman, Kendra?"

"Do you always get your way, playboy?"

"Only with women who know their minds and have autonomy. Those with controlling partners or suffocating rules of Puritanism just see me in their dreams for years to come."

She smirked. "And how would you know that?"

I smiled. "Pour me a refill, would you, Kendra?"

She refilled my cup. It was terrible coffee—old, burnt, and an appalling blend to begin with—but serving me was establishing a pattern for Kendra of doing what I told her to, and receiving my gratitude in return.

"Thank you, love."

"You have an accent," she said.

"That's a good ear you have."

"Where are you from?"

"Sounds like you want to get to know me," I said.

"Just tell me where you're from."

"Lots of places."

Kendra said something in return, but the bell over the door jingled as she spoke, and I turned to look at the new customer, irritated I no longer had the diner to myself.

I have seen many women. From ancient Greece to medieval Scandinavia to nineteenth century Australia—I have seen beauties that defy description in any of the languages I know.

The young woman who walked into the diner was no historic beauty. She was cute enough, but wore unflattering clothes and was rather flat-chested. She wore no apparent makeup, and her brown curls hung free.

Yet she captivated me.

She sat down several stools away from me at the counter, looking weary. Kendra went over and took her order of pie and coffee.

A few moments later, Kendra returned to me, a coy smile on her lips. "I think maybe I *will* invite you over for a drink. What's your poison?"

Still looking at the new girl, I waved a dismissive hand at Kendra. "Really, doll, you must think of your boyfriend."

I rose, coffee in hand, and walked the few paces to the new girl's side.

"Mind if I sit?"

The girl looked up at me, then down at the seat beside her. Then she made a show of glancing about the empty diner. "No other seats suit your fancy?"

"I fancy none so much as this one."

"Very well—it's a free country."

"So they say." I took the seat, then extended my hand, feeling Kendra's eyes boring into me from across the room. "My name is Saul."

The girl hesitated, then gripped my proffered hand. "Jael."

"What a lovely name."

She offered a wry smile and sipped her coffee.

"Really," I said, "it is."

"Yeah, well, it means 'mountain goat.'"

She was trying to throw me off my game.

"Mountain goats can be . . . majestic."

"Give it up, Casanova."

Never.

"Tell me, Jael, what's a girl like you doing out so late?"

"A girl like me?"

"A respectable, wholesome sort of girl, I mean."

Jael chuckled. "Sir, I think you're barking up the wrong tree."

"*Sir*? How appalling. Do I look old to you? I've been told I appear perpetually shy of thirty."

"You have a way of speaking that makes you seem older. But, anyway, I'm too young for you in any case."

"How old are you?"

"Don't you know better than to ask a woman that?"

"I know no such thing. And, anyway, I don't know yet if you are a woman. Perhaps you're an ancient looking ten-year-old."

"Not quite."

"I would guess you're eighteen or nineteen. I'm quite good at guessing ages. How close am I?"

Jael said nothing, but a certain twitch of her lips told me I was at least adjacent to the mark.

"You know, Jael, you look quite tired."

"Meaning what? I should go to bed and sleep— with you?"

I made a show of shock. "No such thing. I was going to ask if I could buy you a refill. Or maybe we could go to a proper coffee shop. I fear the coffee here is actually rat poison."

"Sorry. I need to get going soon."

"Oh—where to?"

"I'm afraid I don't feel comfortable sharing that with a stranger."

"Stranger? Who's a stranger? I'm Saul—don't you remember?"

"Well, Saul, it takes more than a few minutes for me to consider someone more than a passing acquaintance."

"Then give me a few minutes more."

She glanced at her watch, a cheap plastic thing. "I'll be leaving at the bottom of the hour."

I consulted my own timepiece, a Patek Philippe that night. "Six minutes. That's enough time to get to know a person, don't you think?"

"Hardly."

"You don't yet know how fast I can talk."

"You're talking fast enough already," she said.

"Well, I used to work as an auctioneer."

"Really?"

"No. But I was a politician once."

"Yeah?"

"Sort of. It was a long time ago."

"Well, now I really can't trust you."

"What, because I was a politician? Oh, ignore that—that was a lie, too."

"So, either you're a politician, or you've lied to me twice? Great, I think I'm beginning to trust you."

"I really do grow on a person, given enough time."

"So does a fungus."

"Ouch. Such a sharp tongue."

"Sorry," she said. "That was unnecessary."

"I'm afraid I'll only forgive you if you have coffee with me."

"We're having coffee now."

"Nonsense. This is rat poison, as I said. Surely this town has a good coffee shop."

"Just down the road."

"Perfect."

"I recommend *you* try it," she said, "but *I* really do have to be going."

"Oh, no, we were just getting to know each other."

She shook her head. "This is a small town. Our standards for knowing someone are pretty high."

"Well, you know, I was thinking of staying in the area for a while. Maybe we could meet another time."

"Maybe," she said, but was not convincing.

"What's your number?"

"Ten."

"You live in the wrong era to make that joke."

"I'm an old soul."

"Well now," I said, "that's something we have in common."

"You're an old soul?"

"Oh, trust me, if I have a soul, it's certainly very old."

"If?"

"It's been debated. Soul detection is such tricky business."

"I see."

I rose, and hurried over to a sour Kendra at the register. I paid for my bill and Jael's. Then I returned to her side.

"Well, I paid your tab, so I'm afraid you owe me now."

Jael took out a few bills and placed them on the counter. She smirked, then turned and made for the door.

"I'll be seeing you, Jael."

Raising a hand over her shoulder in farewell, she pushed through the door and disappeared into the night.

3

I died in A.D. 20-something. I was not tracking years with the Julian or Gregorian calendars at that time, but I know it was a couple decades before the Roman Conquest of Britain.

Welsh by birth, my name in life was Morcant.

It is difficult for me to think of myself as synonymous with that old Morcant. The short life of that no-account barbarian is truly ancient history. Actually, it is not even that—it is prehistoric to the annals of Britannia.

My strength is that of many men, but my mind experienced no great improvement after my death, so there is much of the past two thousand years I cannot recall. I sometimes confuse real experiences with movies I have seen, so far removed am I from ancient and medieval times.

One might think I would be the smartest or richest man in the world—but they would be placing far too much confidence in my work ethic and intelligence. I am, it is true, a billionaire, but I would never have acquired such wealth in one lifetime—or even ten. I am wealthy based simply on the fact that paltry investments can become quite significant over the course of a few hundred years.

Similarly with knowledge, I could not help picking up some things over the millennia, even if I was not actively studying. Indeed, I spent the first few hundred years of my living-death illiterate, and only picked up the skills of reading and writing through a combination of immersion and boredom.

But I never placed great stock in wealth or knowledge, except insofar as they allowed me to pursue pleasure, my one true aim in existence.

Valuable above all else to me were the bodies of bodaciously buxom beauties.

My lovers have been commoners, noblewomen, prostitutes, and even queens. Had I the ability to beget children, I could have been the father of nations.

The first girl I ever truly fancied led to my death. She was a mysterious mute among the captives my tribe took in a night raid upon another village. I had a wife already, but she was unattractive, given to me in a marriage of convenience.

My father was an elder in the tribe, and he gave me leave to take a second wife, as the first had borne me no children.

He said, "One with a barren womb, the other with no tongue. Maybe together they will be a whole wife."

So, I took the pale beauty from among the captives and brought her into my home.

"You are my woman now," I said. "Do you understand?"

She stared with unreadable dark eyes. I saw no fear there, but I saw no positive expression either.

My first wife was not at all pleased to see her.

"You choose the fairest girl for our slave? Is it because you would lie with her?"

"She is not a slave, but my new wife. You will treat her as such."

"You are a cruel husband to me."

"And you are a barren, sharp-tongued woman. Maybe this girl will have an open womb. At the least, she has no tongue to lash me."

My wife stormed out of the hut.

I pulled the girl to me then and kissed her. She kissed me back, then moved to press her lips against my cheek, and then my neck.

Then she bit me.

With a startled cry, I tried to push her from me, but she clung to me like a leech. And like a leech, she sucked the blood from my veins.

I reached for the knife at my belt, but the girl seized my wrist in a grip strong and cold as iron. I continued to struggle, but she proved stronger than any mortal human I had ever encountered.

As the blood left my body at an alarming rate, I fell to the dirt-and-rush floor of my hut, the girl on top of me, her mouth still clamped fast to my neck.

I lay there, no longer struggling, as darkness encroached upon my vision.

At some point, the girl pressed her wrist against my lips. She had opened a vein in her forearm, and I could not resist as her blood flowed into my mouth.

And I awoke.

Cold fire coursed through my body, and my mind buzzed with the shock of dark lightning. I was on my feet, then upon the rafters, my every movement magnified tenfold in speed and power.

After that, my memory is hazy. I think my new wife and I killed some people in my tribe. The others drove us away, and we harassed them in the nights that followed. I guess we eventually won, killing some and causing the rest to flee the area.

We soon moved on, seeking fresh blood.

Some years later, we parted ways.

I heard she was killed—bodily destroyed, I should say—not long after Christianity came to Britain. I did not hear how it happened, but, of course, it must have been by burning—either fire or the sun—or being pierced through the heart with wood or silver.

I went on to fight in many wars, valued highly for my incredible strength and my apparent imperviousness to injury. I fought as an independent mercenary, a champion, and I only joined a fray or mission at night, as exposure to the sun seared my flesh.

War and death, blood and women—such was the sum of my "life" in those days.

4

I asked around for Jael, but folk in the little town of Silver Plume, Colorado, seemed reticent to divulge information to a pale, nightwalking stranger who wore black and drove a hearse.

Ordinarily, I would have moved right along. The town had little to offer, and I had only stopped the other night because I was hungry.

Of course, I could not digest the food on any diner menu. But diners have waitresses, and Kendra had seemed a willing enough appetizer.

Then Jael had walked in, and I had forgotten all about my hunger—for calories, at least.

I was not sure what about her intrigued me, but I had to stay and find out.

In the days that followed, I remained in the area. I got a room at the Historic Windsor, as it was the only hotel in town.

I liked the vintage feel of the place, though I missed some modern conveniences—like an unshared bathroom. But my room did have a minifridge where I could keep some blood packs fresh.

Mainly, though, I stayed in the parking lot. In my own car.

I never use hotel beds for sleeping. No two-star, communal DNA collection apparatus for me. No risking an encounter with other blood-suckers in the form of bedbugs.

My bed of choice is a coffin. And, quite naturally, I keep that in my hearse. I often moonlight as a mortician, which, in the minds of many, goes some way toward explaining my paleness and eccentricities.

I ventured out into the town around noon on Saturday—after applying a high-SPF sunscreen and donning long sleeves, kidskin gloves, a fedora, and sunglasses. Leaving the hearse parked at the hotel, I walked about the town, reveling in the thrill of danger that came with venturing about under the sun.

Tucked neatly into the Rockies off of Interstate 70, the town is quaint, I suppose. An old mining town, apparently. Population: maybe a couple hundred.

It surely attracts tourists at the right times, but the town seemed very quiet that day.

My walk soon took me beyond the limits of Silver Plume and into the adjacent Georgetown, though I had only gone two or three miles.

As I strode past a gas station, I saw a short girl with brown curls, standing by an ugly old sedan at the pump.

Her back was toward me, but it could be *her.*

I adjusted course and hurried toward her. When I was within a few paces, I caught her scent.

"Hello, Jael."

She turned to face me. She stared hard, seeming not to recognize me. It might have been because of my hat and glasses, but I have found that my face always seems to allude people's memories.

"It's Saul," I said. "From the diner."

"Oh. Yes. I remember."

The pump clicked, and she removed the nozzle from her car. "I'm surprised you stuck around."

"I told you I'd be seeing you. You made quite an impression on me."

Though she tried to hide it, I noted her slight blush.

I decided to play with a bit more candor than I used with most girls. She seemed the sort for that approach.

"Listen, Jael, I really would love to have coffee with you. Forgive my forwardness, but you intrigue me. I hate to immediately rush away when I encounter someone interesting. One meets so few people who register as unique from the masses."

Jael looked me up and down, as though she could evaluate my character through some telltale sign in outward appearance. Then she glanced into her car, and I realized there was someone in the passenger seat. A redheaded chick, maybe a few years older than Jael.

"My sister and I were going to get lunch. If she's OK with it, you can join us. We wouldn't want you thinking the folk of Georgetown-Silver Plume are entirely cold-shouldered."

"Splendid."

Jael opened the car door and spoke with her sister.

A moment later, she looked back at me. "Is your car here or in Silver Plume?"

I nodded in the westerly direction from which I had come.

"OK," Jael said, "hop in. We'll drive you to the coffee shop."

5

Meals. Always a sticky situation for those like me.

I can drink water, black coffee, and a few other non-caloric beverages. But I become sick if I give my body solid food or caloric liquids other than blood.

Over the centuries, however, I have gotten better about holding food down longer. Like a bulimic, I have to vomit after meals, but I can often go an hour or more before my stomach becomes too upset.

I typically keep a supply of blood on hand. It is usually animal blood, which is sufficient to get me through lean times. But nothing except human blood can fully satisfy.

Normally, I obtain this without any death. Amorous encounters often allow me to disguise a tiny puncture mark in the neck with a hickey. But the small amount of blood I surreptitiously obtain is rarely satisfactory.

Of course, some girls are on board for the real thing, imagining we are enacting some gothic fantasy. There is, thankfully, an increasing number of such women.

The last time I killed, the woman was a killer of sorts herself, so I was only adhering to what she had established as acceptable practice.

Sitting in the back seat of Jael's car, I pushed thoughts of killing from my mind. I was there to have lunch with Jael, not have her for lunch.

"I'm surprised I didn't remember you right away," Jael said. "People say I have a photographic memory."

"Well, I'm very unphotogenic."

As we pulled out of the gas station, Jael nodded to her sister. "Saul, this is Kezia. Kez, Saul."

Kezia turned partway in her seat and eyed me with apparent suspicion. "What brings you to the area?"

"Oh, I'm on a vacation of sorts. Road-tripping America."

"What do you do?"

"I'm a mortician."

The girl visibly shuddered. "So, you deal with a lot of dead bodies?"

"Oh, yes," I said, "a good many."

"How do you stand it?"

"Well, it comes quite naturally to me, I suppose."

"How do you mean?"

"I feel rather dead myself."

Kezia arched an eyebrow. "What do you mean?"

"Unfulfilled, I mean. I've always felt unfulfilled. Helping people find rest and peace is somewhat fulfilling, I've found."

Jael looked at me in the rearview. "Where's your next stop when you move on?"

"Oh, wherever fancy or circumstance takes me at the time. I haven't even decided when I will be moving on yet. I rather like what I've seen of the town."

"Really?"

"Yes, truly."

Jael turned the car into the parking lot of a coffee shop. "I know it's lunchtime, but this place has great coffee and bagels."

"Perfectly fine by me. I typically work night shifts, so conventional ideas about which hours or foods constitute breakfast and lunch are meaningless to me."

"I often work nights as well," Jael said.

"Oh, where at?"

"The police station. I'm a dispatcher."

"Ah, how interesting."

Jael opened her door. "Not really. Again, small town."

We went inside, and I insisted on paying for the girls' orders. For myself, I got coffee that was not half bad for a small town, and a regrettable bagel.

We sat in a corner of the shop beyond the reach of the sun, and I cautiously removed my hat and glasses.

"So, Jael, what sort of 'uninteresting' calls do you deal with as a dispatcher?"

Jael sipped her coffee, which she had ruined with sugar. "Some wrecks, or vehicles broken down or trapped by snow. The occasional theft— mostly just kids. When the tourists are around, we even get some reports of bigfoot or werewolf sightings."

"Really?"

"Yeah. Keeps us amused."

"It always amazes me, the things people believe. Ape- or wolf-men, blood-sucking monsters—such silliness."

"Yeah. I think we have some pranksters in the area. We've seen 'bigfoot' tracks, but they were very likely hoaxes."

"People always want to believe in something outside the ordinary," I said.

"Is there nothing extraordinary that you believe yourself?"

"Hmm . . . I suppose I do believe there might be an honest politician somewhere out there. Just a young one, mind you, in an isolated part of the globe."

Jael laughed, and Kezia gave a weak smile.

"But, of course," I said, "I've never actually encountered one, and I've traveled much of the world."

"As a mortician?"

"I studied abroad. Also, I often take extended, international vacations. I've made my millions, so my work is mainly to stave off boredom."

"You've made millions as a mortician?"

"Well, I've served as coroner for royalty in the past. But, primarily, my wealth came from lucky investments. Some gambling, too."

I noticed Kezia eyeing me, as if looking for indications of my wealth. Everything I wore was quite expensive and professionally tailored, but it was not elaborate or flashy, so the subdued luxury eluded the casual observer. The Jaeger-LeCoultre might have satisfied Kezia, but I always wore my watches on the inside of my wrist, so she probably could not see the dial at the moment.

But I could not help showing off. I had practiced sleight of hand tricks for hundreds of years, so my skill bordered upon real magic.

"Kezia, I see you're skeptical. Perhaps you think I'm exaggerating my status. I think you will find something under your coffee cup."

Kezia lifted her cup, and there lay a gold coin.

"Ancient Roman," I said. "I forget exactly how much it's worth, but it would cause many collectors to drool. Keep it."

Kezia quickly pushed it toward me. "Oh, no, I can't."

I disappeared the coin, then, in the most basic of moves, pulled it out from behind Jael's ear. "Ah! Well, I guess it's yours now."

Jael smiled, shaking her head. "Don't be silly. There's no way I'm taking that if it's real."

"I assure you, it's real." I placed it on the table. "I also assure you that I will not pick it up again. So, if one of you doesn't take it, an employee here will receive a ridiculous tip."

Jael frowned. "Why would you want to give that away?"

"I have many. I picked them up when they were worth a lot less. Inflation, you know."

Before Jael could say anything, Kezia changed the subject. "What's your interest in Jael?"

So. Assuming the role of direct and abrasive big sister.

I thought of charming or hypnotizing her. But I do not like using my uncanny powers in my interactions with women. It feels unsportsmanlike.

"Well, Kez, I just want to talk. It's not often that I meet interesting people."

"What's interesting about her?"

I looked at Jael as I answered Kezia's question. "Something intangible. Nebulous. An intriguing soul-mark."

"Sounds hippie-dippie," Kezia said.

Jael waved her hand between me and Kezia. "Um, hello? You guys are talking about me like I'm not here."

I smiled. "Please, feel free to shut either of us up. Am I insane for wanting to get to know you, or is your sister crazy for standing in my way?"

"Neither of you are crazy. Kez is just protective. We don't get many strangers in this town, outside of tourist season."

"Well, how can I make myself less of a stranger?"

Jael glanced over at Kezia, as though anticipating resistance to her incoming suggestion. "You could come to dinner tomorrow night."

Kezia stiffened. "J, I'm not sure Dad would—"

"Oh, he won't mind. He'll appreciate the company." She looked to me. "What do you say?"

"I say you're very kind, and I gladly accept the invitation."

"We're vegetarians. I hope that's OK."

"Of course. I have some dietary restrictions myself."

"Oh? Anything we should be aware of when preparing a meal?"

"I'm allergic to garlic."

"Good to know."

Kezia took what seemed a very intentional bite of her everything bagel.

"Our house is outside of Silver Plume," Jael said, "off of Silver Valley Road as you head west along Clear Creek, past Deadman Gulch, but before the road merges with East Bakerville—"

"Maybe you should draw me a map."

Jael drew a map on a napkin and told me the time of their Sunday night dinner. Then we finished our coffee, and the girls left.

Exiting the shop with hat and sunglasses in place, I stepped behind a dumpster and vomited the bagel I had forced down.

I threw up some blood along with it. But I knew it was only pigs' blood. It had been too long since I had drunk any of the good stuff.

My mouth began to water as I thought of how Jael's blood would taste.

6

I had not yet decided if I would convert Jael. It had been decades since I had last turned anyone, and there were less than a dozen of my second-hand progeny still walking to and fro upon the earth.

In the early days, I converted many. Whenever I encountered a great beauty, I wanted her around forever. But my blood-begotten mistresses often developed minds of their own after their conversions, and I rarely had an undead lover for long. And having one's exes around forever is nightmarish enough to drive a man to desperate measures.

Some of them met untimely ends. Not by my hand directly, but I tipped off some of the organizations that hunted "monsters."

I hardly turned anyone anymore. The last time had actually been to save someone's life. A moment of weakness.

I knew, at least, I would not destroy Jael. Maybe Kezia. But I liked Jael. I would feed upon her—possibly convert her—but not kill her in the traditional sense. If I drained her, I would give her my blood in return, and she would experience the world in a whole new way.

But I remained undecided. I would allow for a bit more consideration before I determined if she was truly someone I wanted around for centuries or even millennia.

After the sun dipped below the mountains Sunday evening, I rose from the coffin in the back of my hearse. I climbed into the front seat and drove toward the address Jael had given me.

Standing on the porch with flowers and an expensive bottle of wine, I knocked twice.

The voice behind the door was muffled, but I thought it was Jael's. "Door's unlocked!"

I frowned. She had not technically invited me inside, and being such as I am, it was impossible for me to step past the threshold until she did.

"Come on in!"

There it was.

Smiling, I opened the door and stepped into the living room.

"I'm in the kitchen! Sorry, I have my hands full. Kezia is upstairs, and Dad is in the study."

I followed the sound of her voice into the next room. She stood before a steaming pot on the stovetop, stirring vigorously with a wooden spoon. She wore a floral apron, and her brown curls were pulled back from her rosy face in a loose ponytail.

"I can't stop stirring this fudge for a few minutes," she said. "Sorry."

"Why on earth would you apologize for making fudge?" I smiled. "I wasn't sure if you drank wine, so I brought flowers too. But don't worry, they're not used."

"Used?"

"In a funeral. I'm a mortician, remember? Just a little joke."

"Ah, right. Well, thank you very much. You didn't need to do that."

I set the wine and flowers down, then leaned my hip against the counter as I watched her.

A shy smile tugged at the corners of her mouth. "I don't know what you're looking at. I'm a mess. This is what you get for being early."

I chuckled. "Women never seem to realize how attractive they are with the flush of exertion in their cheeks—yet they imitate that with the makeup they apply."

"I've never thought about it that way. But, then, I don't wear makeup much."

"With beauty like yours," I said, "it would be a redundancy."

"Flattery will get you nowhere."

"Flattery has gotten me many places. But, in this case, I'm restricting myself to the truth."

She chuckled. "Whatever would you do without your tongue?"

"Oh, I would certainly have to give up on life at that point. 'Death and life are in the power of the tongue: and they that love it shall eat the fruit thereof.'"

Even a devil can quote Scripture for his own purposes.

A man in a wheelchair rolled into the kitchen at that moment. Jael's father, I presumed.

"Oh—Saul, this is my dad. Dad, Saul."

He extended a hand, and I shook it.

"Cold hands you've got there," he said. "But I guess you know what they say about cold hands."

Of course I knew, but I habitually deny knowing much of anything, as two thousand years grant one a suspicious amount of knowledge.

"No," I said. "What do they say?"

"A warm heart, that's what they say."

"Ah, well, who am I to disagree with They?"

The man laughed. "I'm Peter, by the way—not just Dad."

"Pleased to meet you, sir."

Kezia sauntered into the room. "Ah, it's the wayfaring stranger. J, I thought you were gonna give him the address of the old abandoned house."

Jael rolled her eyes. "Save it, Kez. Now come help me with pouring this."

Peter leaned back in his wheelchair and gave me an evaluating glance-over. "So. The girls tell me you're a mortician."

"That's right," I said.

"Not too much need of a mortician around here."

That could always be remedied.

"I'm not trying to set up a local practice. I'm on a bit of a sabbatical right now. Seeing the country."

"Where are you from, originally?"

I almost answered truthfully. But it is my habit to lie about my roots, and not use the same tale too often.

"I'm from Ireland," I said.

"Funny, I would've never guessed Irish from your accent."

"No, I've lived in too many countries for my accent to be any one thing. I've lived in England, France, Romania, Albania, Greece, and other places."

"That's a lot for anyone," Peter said, "let alone someone your age."

I smiled. "Yes, I've lived enough for many lifetimes."

"Have you been a mortician in all those places?"

"No. I've been a nightwatchman, bouncer, bartender, magician, card dealer, and a few other things."

"Well. You certainly *have* lived a lot. You must not stay at one thing very long."

"I do get bored quite easily."

"You hear that, J?" Kezia smirked at her sister. "Not good hubby material."

Jael blushed, Peter reprimanded Kezia, and the dinner preparations proceeded.

Kezia was really beginning to get on my nerves. I had pretty well decided I would kill her.

Peter was an OK sort. I had no real interest in killing him. But he might wish to die after he saw what I would do to his daughters.

Jael took off her apron. "Kez, will you set the table while I go upstairs and clean up before dinner?"

"You look fine."

"Please, Kez."

"Go on. I've got it."

Jael hurried away, and I watched her go. And I made my decision.

Yes. She will be mine.

Kezia turned to me. "Well, stranger, want to make yourself useful?"

"Actually, I was hoping you could direct me to the bathroom."

"It's the door to the left of the stairs."

"Thank you."

I left the kitchen and made my way toward the stairs. Once out of sight, I darted up the steps with my unnatural speed and was at Jael's door in an instant.

I could hear her moving about. Could smell her.

I opened the door and stepped into her room.

The door's hinges were apparently well-oiled, for they made no sound when I opened the door, nor when I shut it.

Jael stood before a mirror positioned atop her dresser, putting on earrings. It must have been an old mirror with a silver backing, for no reflection of me appeared as I silently stepped up behind Jael.

She glimpsed me then in her periphery, and gave a sharp gasp as she spun.

I stood before her, saying nothing, my face revealing nothing.

Jael drew back, but immediately encountered the dresser. "What on earth are you doing in here?"

"I want you, Jael."

"Sir, you have very much misjudged me. Now leave my room immediately."

I continued to stare, and she could surely see the hunger in my eyes then.

"I said leave. *Now.*"

"No."

I saw then that she would scream. Springing forward, I clamped a hand over her mouth. Her back struck the dresser, and she yelped, the sound muffled against my palm.

She lashed out at me, but I caught her by the wrist, spun her around, and wrenched her arm behind her back, still covering her mouth with my other hand. She whimpered, but could not struggle without inflicting great pain on her shoulder.

"I think I will convert you," I said. "Then we can take care of your sister together."

She tried to bite my hand, and I laughed.

"Not yet, love. Too much of your own blood still in your veins."

Gripping her mouth and jaw firmly, I tilted her head to one side, exposing her neck, where her jugular vein and carotid artery pumped heartily.

Then I bit her.

She cried out, but the sound only escaped through her nostrils.

Her hot blood flooded my mouth.

An immediate wave of nausea gripped my stomach. The blood triggered my gag reflexes, and I stumbled backward, releasing Jael.

I fell to my knees, spewing blood. I choked and struggled to breathe.

I knew what this was, having experienced it several times before.

"You—you are *Christian*!"

Jael screamed. She did not dare run for the door, as I was between her and it. But she backed into the farthest corner of the room, eyes wide with terror.

Feet pounded the stairs. That would be Kezia.

Spitting out the last of the noxious blood, I stood.

Well. This had not gone at all according to plan.

I thought of trying to salvage a bit of my plan by killing Kezia. But that would be almost pointless, as I would not be able to drain her if she was a Christian also.

I could not drink the blood of one who was chosen by God, indwelt by the Spirit, and had spiritually drunk the blood of Christ. Nor could such a one drink my blood and thereby become like me.

Choking back bile, I glared at the cowering saint.

I could kill Christians, but I could not make them mine. Bought with blood already, they were separated from me. If they merely claimed Christianity as a cultural identity, there was no issue. I could even drain and turn some so-called ministers. But if a person was truly of the chosen, they could not be my blood-get.

The bedroom door flew open and Kezia rushed in, chef's knife in hand.

She saw me, the blood on the carpet, and Jael in the corner with blood on her blouse.

I was very grateful for my inhuman speed, for I needed it to avoid the redhead's berserker rage and maniacal knife-slashing.

Darting to the window, I opened it and leapt out.

The two-story fall was nothing for one such as I. Landing on my feet, I turned and looked back up.

Kezia leaned out the window. She hurled the knife at me, but it was a laughable throw.

She then proceeded to hurl many vicious and vile curses at me.

So. Not a perfect Christian, at least.

Why, yes, Kez, I will *go to the place where the worm dieth not—just as soon as one of you bloody Way-followers manages to punch my ticket.*

I turned and strode toward my hearse, Kez's curses following me all the way.

7

I glanced at the rearview mirror in time to see Peter roll out onto the porch with a shotgun. I could not hear what he was shouting, but I could imagine. He let off a hasty shot as I sped down the driveway.

It missed, and I turned onto Silver Valley Road and accelerated.

I drove west a short ways, then turned left onto Stevens Gulch Road. A few minutes later, I veered off the road and eased the hearse into the trees. I did not make it far before encountering trunks I could not skirt, but it was far enough that some firs obscured the view from the road.

I would have to leave my coffin, and my garment bag of fine clothes would be of little use for the time. So, I took only my bugout bag, filled as it was with toiletries, money, practical clothing, and suchlike.

I owned a safehouse less than a hundred miles away. It would not take long to reach it, and I could pick up a new identity, car, and whatever else I needed there.

But I was not ready to leave yet.

Remembering Kezia's mention of an abandoned house, I decided to look for that. It might prove to be a suitable place to hold up for a short while.

I crossed a creek a short distance from the road, and continued deeper into the forest. I was unconcerned about leaving a scent trail, as dogs would absolutely refuse to follow the spore of a monster such as I. And even if the police did find me, they would not be showing up with wooden stakes and silver blades.

There were a few organizations that recognized and hunted us, but a police report about a stranger biting a girl would not be enough to deploy their forces. I would have to start draining people before that would happen.

I knew I should leave. Genuine Christians were trouble, and nothing could be gained by fixating on one of their saintly little virgins. I should leave town immediately. Forget about Jael.

There were millions of sluts in the world, with gluts of blood for the taking.

But, if I was being honest, I realized that was precisely the intrigue of the perky little demoiselle that was Jael. The ingenuous naïf was off-limits— which made her exactly what I could not walk away from.

Easy bints are tuppence a pair. No true value there.

Why should I waste my time on something any man-jack could score without any great effort?

No, broads like Kendra from the diner were a bad habit. An embarrassing diversion. Junk food.

I wanted the food of angels. Manna and a cup overflowing.

I wanted a body that had been a sacred temple.

Christians speak of the perseverance of the saints. "Once saved, always saved."

Well, we would see about that.

Jael would be my test subject for the doctrine.

Put on your armor, little saint—the fiery darts cometh.

8

"You must suffer me to go my own dark way."

More than a hundred years ago, I heard someone say that, and it stuck with me. Became one of my mottos.

I would bloody well go my own way—dark, dim, dazzling or otherwise—for who was there on this earth to stop me?

Any fool who did not suffer me to do my own will, well, they would *suffer* me.

I am Morcant. Virgins' bane, killer of conquerors, drinker of royal blood.

"His young ones suck up blood; and where the slain are, there is he."

Eventually, I came upon the abandoned house I sought. Situated down a winding dirt road on a property long neglected, it looked perfect for the setting of a ghost story—and little else.

There was no front door. I crossed the creaking porch and stepped across the threshold, needing no invitation here.

I made my way into the kitchen. One door there opened to a walk-in pantry. Might be a good place to sleep, though a closet upstairs should prove a more comfortable option for avoiding the light of day.

The other door wailed as I flung it wide. The musty odor that wafted up reminded me of the Ukrainian catacombs in which I had resided for a time.

I made my way down the old wooden steps. A quick sweep of the cellar revealed nothing but bare shelves, old spider webs, and what might be a rat's nest in the corner.

This would do just fine as a holding cell.

I dropped my bag on the floor. I took from it the thermos keeping a couple pints of blood cool, drained it in a single draft, and cursed the necessary temperature of the thing.

I wanted fresh blood. Hot, sweet, veinous O Negative from a young female would be delightful.

Not this cold, coagulating, mobile blood bank fare.

Well. I would soon fulfil my desire, once I turned Jael into a free agent.

I shoved the empty thermos back into my bag, and took out a torch. I clicked it on and off to check the batteries, then slipped it into my pocket beside my knife.

I left the cellar, strode from the house, and rushed through the woods faster than the bats that darted about in the darkness in search of their prey.

I set my face toward Jael's house.

There was no police vehicle—undercover or otherwise—on or near the property. So, the cops had either deemed my return unlikely, or perhaps the family had not even called the police. The latter seemed unlikely, but one could never tell with country folk. More than a few had the "I am 9-1-1" mentality.

In any case, this simplified matters for me.

I walked right on up the driveway.

Theirs was the only house within a mile's radius, so I did not worry about nosy neighbors.

When I stepped onto the porch, I knew I could not enter the house. I was uninvited, spiritually speaking, and so my way was barred.

A house swept clean, yet not empty.

No matter.

I sat in the rocking chair on the far end of the porch. And I started singing.

"'I'm just a poor, wayfaring stranger . . .'"

I sang loud enough that someone inside would surely hear me. And the chair was not visible from any of the windows, so someone would probably come out eventually.

To his credit, when Peter opened the door, he rolled out and fired off his shotgun with surprising speed.

But the shot splintered an empty chair.

I was beside him, and as he looked up, I seized the barrel of the gun and wrenched it from his hands. Then I grabbed him by the front of his shirt, lifted him from the chair, and hurled him from the porch.

The banshee Kezia issued forth from the house then, brandishing a weapon far more deadly than her father's shotgun: a sharpened broom handle.

So, perhaps she guessed at my nature. She was, after all, the only one in the family to treat me with some hostility from the very beginning.

ASHER ALLEN

She charged at me with her makeshift spear, but I easily dodged to one side, then kicked her in the back as she careened past me. She stumbled off the porch and sprawled on the front lawn.

I sprang after her, seized her by the hair, and yanked her to her feet, swatting the broom handle from her grasp with my free hand.

Peter was crawling toward his shotgun, but I knew he would not risk a shot while I held his daughter. And even if he did, it would only be a bit of pain for me, with the wounds healing almost immediately.

Jael rushed out the front door, but stopped short when she saw the situation.

I held Kezia's hair above her head, so she had to stand on her toes to prevent it being ripped out by the roots. She squirmed and swore some, but she was not going anywhere.

As Jael stared at me, I flipped open my pocket knife and held the tip against Kezia's back.

"Good evening, Jael. In case there is any confusion on the part of you or your father, let me make this very clear: only one thing will stop me from cutting Kezia's spinal column from her body—and that is you marching down those steps and taking her place as my hostage. Immediately."

Peter tried to stop her. Said some words and crawled toward her. But both of us ignored him as we kept our gazes locked upon each other. What I saw in her eyes did not seem to be fear, but restrained fury.

And then she stepped from the porch.

"J, don't listen to—"

I pulled Kezia's hair a bit harder to stop her tongue.

Jael crossed the few paces between us, then stood before me. Her hair was a mess, and she wore a frumpy T-shirt and pajama bottoms. And she was stunning.

I released Kezia's hair and shoved her aside. Reaching out, I grabbed Jael by the arm and pulled her forward.

"Now listen. I want you to come along peaceably. I can render you unconscious if I have to, but I like to think all three of you will comply with my wishes, because you know I will kill the other two if any one of you plays the hero."

"What do you want?" Her tone was cold and surprisingly calm.

"I want you to take my hand and walk with me. And I want your family to go back into the house and keep their mouths shut, if they ever want to see you again."

I extended my hand.

"Jael, no!" Peter reached vainly for his daughter.

Jael stared at my hand, and I saw a flicker of indecision in her expression.

Then she took my hand.

9

After a final reminder to Peter and Kezia that I would immediately kill Jael if any attempt at rescue was made, I led Jael away through the forest.

Her small hand trembled in my grip, but she did not struggle as I guided her through the darkness.

"What are you going to do with me? My family is not rich."

"I am not holding you for ransom."

"Then . . . what?"

"I fancy you," I said.

"Fancy me?"

"Love, if you like."

"This is not love, Saul. This is kidnapping."

"No. You can run back home right now if you want."

"But you will kill my family if I do."

"Yes."

"So," she said, "you are forcing me to this against my will."

"You still have your free will. If you can live with the consequences of your actions, you can return. I may be strongly influencing you, but you still have a choice."

"This is the furthest thing from love, Saul."

"My name is Morcant."

"What do you intend to do with me, Morcant?"

"Talk."

"Just talk?"

"For now," I said.

"We could have done that at the house."

"I was uninvited from your home."

"Because you *bit* me."

"Anyway, your sister is a pest. I want to be alone with you."

"Please don't do this."

"Pleading will get you nowhere, Jael. You will not dissuade me."

She exhaled a shaky breath. I thought she would say more, but she remained silent for the rest of the trek to the abandoned property.

Once in the house, I clicked on my torch—not for my sake, but for hers—and illuminated the way to the kitchen. I opened the cellar door and shined the light upon the steps.

"Go on down."

Without a word, she obeyed, and I followed her down, shutting the door behind me.

Only when I shined the light full upon Jael there in the cold subterranean room did I feel a twinge of guilt.

She stood there in bare feet and short sleeves, arms hugging herself, shivering.

Placing the torch on its end with the beam illuminating the ceiling to reflectively light the whole room, I opened my bugout bag and took out socks and a denim jacket. I tossed them to Jael, and she quickly put them on.

I took a canteen from the bag and placed it on the floor.

"There is water in that. Later I will give you the animals I catch, after I drink their blood. You will stay here until you apostatize."

She blinked several times. "You . . . drink blood . . . and you want me to deny Christ?"

"Yes."

"Why?"

"Why what?"

"Both," she said.

"I drink blood because, as your Scriptures say, 'the life of the flesh is in the blood.' And you must deny Christ so that I may drink your blood, taking your life and giving you my blood and life in return. Then you can live forever."

"I don't understand."

I leaned back against the cold wall, folding my arms. "You are a blood descendant of Adam and Eve, yes?"

Jael folded her own arms. "Yes."

"So, you inherited their sin-fouled blood. You will live a short life and die accursed."

"That would be true," she said, "but Jesus took my curse of sin upon himself, and gives me his pure blood and righteousness in return. I will live forever with him when I pass on from this life to the next."

"Sure. You are blood-bound and transformed by him. But I would have you recant so that *I* may be your 'bridegroom of blood.'"

"Never."

"You would be immortal, Jael."

"I will put on immortality at the resurrection of the dead."

"You could be undead now."

"Are you saying you cannot be killed?"

Though she appeared nonchalant, I had heard the slight strain of tone indicative of the weight she placed on the question.

I smiled. "I am saying I cannot die naturally. And it is very difficult to kill me. I am nearly two thousand years old, Jael. I was reborn not long before your Christ was killed."

"He lives," she said. "He defeated death and reigns eternally. Every enemy will be put under his feet."

She stood there in the dim light with her own feet in a wide stance, arms still folded, back straight.

She was beautiful, even in her opposition to my will. How ravishing she would be upon servile knees, when my will was her desire.

"So, why does your Master tarry, Jael?"

"He is longsuffering, granting salvation to generation after generation. And a thousand years is as a day to him."

"You could live a thousand years as you await his return."

"And then what? Be found a traitor when he comes back? I have already been reborn, and my Master will return as a warrior in blood-drenched robes to destroy such as you."

"Well, the battle has not yet been fought."

"Such arrogance, to defy God."

I smiled. "Such arrogance have *you*, Jael, to defy *me*."

"You see yourself as a god?" Jael said. "Like a man you shall die, and fall like any prince."

"A Scriptural allusion? Psalm 82, I believe? I am quite familiar with the Scriptures after my centuries of literacy. And I can quote much, even without an eidetic memory like you claim to have."

"But you cannot understand it."

"Oh?"

"It is the Holy Spirit who makes the Word truly known."

"So you say. Yet 'the children of this world are in their generation wiser than the children of light.' Your Christ said that."

"But wiser in what way? In gaining and keeping wealth and optimizing comfort and pleasure in this life, maybe. But what about storing up spiritual treasure for the next life?"

"'A fool is full of words,'" I said, quoting Solomon, "'a man cannot tell what shall be; and what shall be after him, who can tell?'"

"God knows, and he has given us his Word."

"Such childlike faith you have. But I fear you are fated for disappointment."

"We will see."

"Yes," I said, "we shall. Or *I* shall, at least. Your life is a mere breath if you do not accept my offer of immortality."

"It is not immortality you offer."

"Perhaps not in the truest sense of the word, but it's as good as you'll ever get."

"So," Jael said, "what are you, exactly? A demon?"

"*Demon*? Well, before being coopted, that Greek word referred to amoral beings somewhere between the status of gods and men. But then when the Hebrews started speaking Greek, they often used the term to refer to the disembodied souls of their Nephilim. And now many of you Christians use it to mean fallen angels, even though your Scriptures say that 'God spared not the angels that sinned, but cast them down to Tartarus.' So, Jael, when you ask if I am a demon, what do you really mean?"

"Are you any of the above?"

"I have been called Nephilim. But I am not the result of 'the sons of God' coming in to 'the daughters of man,' as your Scriptures say. Though perhaps I am, in a sense, descended from the Nephilim by way of blood rites. I really don't know or care."

"How would you describe yourself?"

"A sort of devil, perhaps, in the looser modern sense of the word."

"Do you like what you are?"

"I accept what I am," I said. "I am not so conceded as to think I can change who I am."

"But people change all the time."

"We can evolve somewhat over time, certainly. Adapt to changing circumstances, alter our interests through habit. But if there is such a thing as a soul, that core identity remains what it ever was."

"Only God is immutable," Jael said. "And even if I agree that we can't change the nature of our souls, I know *he* can. When he saves us, we are transformed. Regenerated. Reborn. Given a new spirit."

"And is *that* changeable? Can you give that up and follow another savior?"

"You are no savior," Jael said.

"I can save you from old age. What are you— nineteen? If I replace your blood with mine, you will forever appear as the youthful beauty you are now."

"I don't want that."

"You lie. Everyone wants to be beautiful."

"Some people want to grow older, Lost Boy. We're not all Peter Pan."

"You *would* grow old," I said. "*I* am old. The physical ravages of age are what is eliminated."

"That's unnatural."

"Isn't that what Christians look forward to? New and ageless bodies at the supposed resurrection? I offer that to you now."

"It is the way of devils to offer a pale and premature imitation of what God intends."

"Better pale reality than dazzling fantasy."

"I choose the promises of God rather than those of a devil."

"You will change your mind."

"I will die first," she said.

"If you do not change, then yes, you will die. You will never leave this room if you do not change."

"I pray you will change your mind rather than let me die. But if not, I am willing to suffer for my faith—even to death."

"We will see," I said.

"I mean it."

"We will see."

11

Jael fell silent. Even in the dim light, I saw the glimmer of a tear spilling onto her cheek. But she quickly turned away. She sat in the far corner and pulled her knees up to her chest.

She would break eventually. I doubted she would be inclined to eat the raw flesh of animals I would drain, so she would soon grow hungry. The water in the canteen was mixed with a bit of pig blood, so she might also find that objectionable. But, since I would still be technically providing for her needs, she could not yet accuse me of forcing her to convert.

I wanted her to have as much autonomy as was reasonable, while still ensuring my ultimate goal.

"How can you say you love me?"

She did not look at me when she spoke.

I had no ready response, and she continued.

"You don't know me," she said. "What makes you say you love me?"

"I am drawn to you, and not in a purely physical way. There is something about your spirit—your soul, or whatever you want to call it."

She looked at me then. "If it is my soul you are drawn to, why would you want me to destroy it by denying God?"

"You think your soul would not be attractive without him?"

"I *know* it," she said. "I am just as wretched as you without his transforming grace and love."

"*My* love could transform you."

"Your passion would soon die. What you love about me would be lost. You cannot eat your cake and have it too. You are like Amnon in the Bible. He was obsessed with a virgin he could not rightly have. After he raped her, his infatuation turned to hatred."

"I will not rape you. You will ask me to take you. And you will beg me to drink your blood."

"You do not know me," Jael said.

"I know humans. They all have a breaking point."

"So, you will torture me?"

"Again, I am not making you do anything. You are free to do whatever you like."

"But if I do anything other than what you tell me, you will kill Kez and Dad."

"We've established that, yes."

"Name one thing about me," Jael said.

"What?"

"Apart from my first name and what you can observe, what do you know about me?"

"You are a Christian," I said, "and you work as a police dispatcher."

"How old am I? What is my last name? What kind of music or books or movies do I like? What kind of person am I interested in romantically? What are my hopes and dreams and fears? How did I become who I am today? What happened to my mother? You know nothing about me."

"I recall you mentioning you were a vegetarian. And you can make fudge."

She uttered a mirthless laugh. "You don't even know if the fudge was any good! You tried consuming my blood instead."

"Yes, well, I am confident the fudge was better than your blood. You Christians are made noxious by serving as living temples."

"Being noxious to evil is one of the best compliments you could pay me."

"I suppose it's not actually you that is noxious," I said. "What repulses me is who you have invited in."

"Invited? You make it sound like I did him a favor. Does someone who has drowned and is clinically dead *invite* the lifeguard to save them? Or are they simply amazed to open their eyes and see the savior who snatched them from death and breathed life into them?"

I raised an eyebrow. "Your sins were so great you saw yourself as drowned to death by them?"

"Only in hindsight. At the time, I was happy to go on sinning. A child born blind does not have a concept of how dark and colorless her world is unless one day she is given sight."

"You are still a teenager, by all appearances. What great sins could you have committed?"

"If you were to spit in the face of a criminal, who would blame you? If you spat in the face of your neighbor, that would be much worse. If you spat in the face of a king, that would be a crime so great you would face the death penalty in certain times or places. And even then, the king is a man, who has surely done much wrong himself. But to spit in the face of God? How can you make up for that?"

"Enough talk about God."

"Never enough," she said.

"I strongly advise you stop, if you know what's good for your family."

"So, then, tell me about yourself, Morcant. You say you are ancient. I'm not sure I believe you, but go ahead—dazzle me with tales of distant times and lands. At least one of us should know something about the other."

"I don't like your tone," I said.

"I don't like your existence."

"Not very Christian of you."

"On the contrary," she said, "if you are something non-human as you claim, it's a very Christian sentiment to wish for the demise of evil."

"I was human once."

"And now you are a pathetic creature that kidnaps teenage girls and threatens to murder innocent families."

"I think you should shut up now."

"I think you should drop dead."

"Done it already."

"Then die again and again till it takes."

I sighed. Two thousand years had proven not long enough for me to develop much patience. And it was looking like this girl would try mine and require much.

"Well, Jael, if you won't shut up, why don't you tell me something about yourself, since you don't think I know enough already? You seem well-spoken. You did well in school, I presume? Top of your class?"

Instead of answering, Jael began humming.

I recognized the old Irish tune, and wished she would stop.

She began singing. "'Be Thou my Vision, O Lord of my heart . . .'"

Rop tú mo baile. An ancient *lorica,* a prayer for protection.

I did not burst into flames or recoil. But Christians singing certain hymns did make me feel nauseated.

Jael had a decent voice, and a good deal of heart behind it.

"'Be Thou my battle Shield, Sword for the fight;

"'Be Thou my Dignity, Thou my Delight;

"'Thou my soul's Shelter, Thou my high Tower:

"'Raise Thou me heavenward, O Power of my power.'"

The hymn brought unwanted memories to me. Thoughts of Ireland. Encounters with Dállan Forgaill, Patrick, and other saints.

By the time she stopped singing, I had to swallow back bile that had risen in my throat.

"Finished?"

She started singing another hymn, and I had to leave. I took the cellar steps at a deliberate pace, and shut the door behind me, hoping she had not seen the extent of my discomfort.

For just a moment, I almost reconsidered my plans for her.

But, no, that would not do.

In all things, I would have my way.

12

I paced the living room, out of earshot of the wretched singing.

After only a few minutes, the cellar door screeched on its hinges.

I rushed into the kitchen as Jael stepped from the doorway.

"I didn't say you could leave the cellar."

"Well, you didn't lock me in," Jael said. "And you said I can do whatever I want. Do you intend to hurt my family because I opened an unlocked door?"

"Very well, you can stay out here until the hour before sunrise. Then I will lock you in."

Jael walked over to the counter, brushed away a thick layer of dust, then turned and hopped up to sit on the countertop. She folded her arms and stared at me, one side of her face illuminated by moonlight streaming through the window.

"I'm disappointed in you, Morcant."

I chuckled. "Oh?"

"Kez thought you were no good, but I was holding onto a slight hope that you might be a decent man. Sad to say, my sister has an irritating habit of being right about most things."

"At last, there is something we can agree upon— your sister is irritating."

"Her always being right might be mildly annoying sometimes, but I would not change her. When we were kids, it was a different story. We were arch-rivals. But after our mom died, we grew close. She is truly my best friend now."

"I assume she is a Christian also?"

"Now, yes. But it took the better part of a year to convince both her and Dad that I wasn't crazy for believing in Jesus."

"Not crazy to believe in his existence, perhaps, but I would say you are a fool to ally yourself to him."

"'We are fools for Christ's sake,'" Jael said. "But 'the foolishness of God is wiser than men, and the weakness of God is stronger than men.' 'The preaching of the cross is to them that perish foolishness; but unto us which are saved it is the power of God.'"

"You have memorized some words. Well, so have I."

"They are empty words to one who does not have the Spirit of truth."

"Well, I'm afraid it is not him I want. I want you. I want you to give up this Spirit and be my bride of blood."

"'Ye cannot drink the cup of the Lord, and the cup of devils: ye—'"

"'Ye cannot be partakers of the Lord's table, and of the table of devils.' Yes. I know. And that is why you must give up your Lord."

"You think you can snatch me from his hand? Jesus said, 'I give unto them eternal life; and they shall never perish, neither shall any man pluck them out of my hand.'"

"We shall see," I said.

"He 'will preserve me unto his heavenly kingdom.'"

"You quote the King James translation of your Scriptures. You know I saw the man once? 1625, I believe it was."

"Did you try to drink his blood too?"

"No. Actually, I rarely drink the blood of men. Biting and sucking can be such intimate actions, so I try to limit myself to females."

"You are sick."

"Actually, I never get sick. One of the perks of this undead life."

"Do you ever get disgusted with yourself?"

"I have experienced every emotion. I have felt, heard, and seen everything. And I agree with Solomon—'all is vanity.'"

"Then why do you insist on having me? Is that not also vanity?"

"It is. But some vanities are better than others. 'Drink, and be drunk with love' is a motto I approve."

"And where has it ever gotten you?"

"Nowhere, of course. Life, little Jael, is about taking whatever pleasure you can for as long as it will last. There is no end goal. No trajectory or meaningful story to this life. It is why people drink. Existence is pain, so we drown our senses at every opportunity."

"If existence is pain, why do you continue in this unnaturally long existence of yours?"

"Because," I said, "the alternative to existence is not worth considering. Non-existence? One cannot even properly comprehend what that means, as we must use existing consciousness to reach for that nebulous idea. Non-existence cannot be experienced, only vaguely considered from a state of present existence."

"So, your only purpose is to try to find pleasure in this life. You're, what, a hedonist?"

"You could call me that," I said. "You could call me many things. I have existed too long to fit neatly into one of your little boxes designed to describe the philosophy of such as see only a few fleeting decades."

"If you truly have lived as long as you say, imagine the good you could have accomplished if you sought that rather than your own pleasure."

"If I ever became famous for some good deed, I would be subject to scrutiny. It's difficult to hide the fact that you do not age when you have a population of people tracking your existence through time."

"You could have worked behind the scenes."

"And who says I have not? But, anyway, what would be the point in that? No glory? A waste."

"You really are quite self-absorbed, aren't you?"

"It's the best way to be, I assure you. But what would you know, having not yet lived two decades?"

"The wisdom of the ages is against you in this," she said.

"The 'wisdom' passed down from one short life to another short life. As soon as anyone has lived long enough to potentially start having something close to an original thought, they are on death's door, or their brain is addled by some degenerative illness. And so, time marches on through the recycling of foolish little lives."

"You think you're so smart, don't you?"

"No, actually I think I'm a born fool. But time can force some knowledge and perspective on even an idiot if he lives long enough."

"What if you're wrong in your perspective?"

"Then so what? Everything is meaningless anyway."

"So, you are a nihilist as well as a hedonist?"

"I am many 'ists.' I am complex. You would have quite an interesting existence if you joined me. I could give you the best that this life has to offer—the most expensive homes and cars, the most exotic travel, the finest clothes and jewelry, sex with one who has centuries of experience."

"So," she said, "you can go and do anything in the world, yet you find yourself in little Silver Plume, Colorado. I guess it all gets old after a while, doesn't it?"

"You speak of what you do not know."

"So, tell me I'm wrong. Tell me you aren't still looking for something that will satisfy you. Tell me that's not why you were drawn to me. You secretly hope there is something different about me. Yet what makes me different is what repulses you, even as it calls to your soul."

"I think you should go back to the cellar now."

13

"I want to keep talking to you, Morcant."

"Then change the subject."

"Fine. Why don't you tell me about yourself?"

"What do you want to know?"

"When were you born?"

"I don't know the day, or even the exact year. Several years B.C., though. Then I was reborn in A.D. 20-something."

"Where was this?"

"Wales."

"So," Jael said, "King Arthur. Was he real?"

"Arthur, Arturus, Artorius, Arturius. He was Brenin Arthur to us Welsh, Arthur Gernow in Cornish, Roue Arzhur in Breton. And he was mostly legendary. But there was a man who formed the basis of the myths. I fought against him, alongside the man who would become known as Medraut or Mordred."

"So, you were on the side of evil from the beginning."

I snorted. "Why do you think Mordred was the villain? Because he lost? You know history is written by the victors, right? And the Arthurian legends are not exactly free of fantastical embellishment."

"Arthur fought on the side of Christianity."

"And Christianity has never been on the wrong side of a war?"

"There is rarely a right side in war," Jael said. "Most wars are political, and brought about by a handful of power-hungry officials."

"What are you, some kind of hippie?"

"Do I have to be a hippie to believe war should be a last resort? Tell me you haven't seen wars fought over trivial matters. Tell me you haven't seen thousands die without truly knowing what they were fighting for or why they should hate the men on the other side."

"War is vanity," I said, "like everything else. But it is quite a profitable business for big governments, and it can be quite fun. You don't have to sneak around to do your killing."

"So, you have been a soldier?"

"I have been a mercenary of sorts in the past. I only fought at night, but I could kill like no other, so I received few complaints."

"How many people have you killed?"

I smirked. "Only serial killers keep count."

"Are you not a serial killer?"

"By technical definition, I would be. But I am not a deranged social outcast with mommy issues, who kills to satisfy some sexual fetish. I am simply a predator, killing for calories."

"You said a moment ago that killing could be fun."

"Yes," I said, "but many soldiers would say that much."

"Do you think some of those soldiers might have become serial killers if they hadn't joined the military?"

"Not many. Most of them would find a more acceptable outlet for their bloodlust—hunting, violent games, that sort of thing."

"So, everyone who hunts is satisfying bloodlust?"

"No," I said, "but many are. It's a thrilling thing to take a life, and the degree of satisfaction is often directly tied to the intelligence of the prey."

"What do you mean?"

"I mean that hooking a stupid fish on a line is all some people need, but others need the bloody takedown of a mammal—a deer or boar, for instance. Still others have to hold a human life in their hands and feel the incredible power of ripping that life from this world. And a select few are not even satisfied with life that only meets the lowest standards of humanity. They have no interest in dumb hookers and foolish drug addicts—they must take the life of a worthy opponent. Someone with the potential to defeat the hunter at his own game."

"Are you like that?"

"Weren't you listening? I told you I'm not a serial killer, psychologically speaking. Any human blood will do for me. Dumb hookers are a staple. Even drugs being in a victim's blood does not affect me. Of course, the act of taking blood is more enjoyable if the prey is pretty and female, so call that a standard if you like."

"Do you consider yourself human?"

"I am more than human," I said, "but I do not think I am *less* than human."

"What makes someone human?"

"There is no consensus on the matter. We cannot even decide if it is limited to *homo sapiens*, or if Neanderthals and others should be included."

"What do *you* believe makes someone human?"

"It doesn't matter what I believe. 'Human' is just an invented term for a somewhat agreed-upon collection of beings. The term would be meaningless outside the collective consciousness of those who invented it."

"Would angels and demons understand what the term meant?"

I shrugged. "I suppose."

"But they are not human, are they?"

"What are you driving at, Jael?"

"Well, you said earlier that you were a devil."

"In a loose sense of the word."

"So," she said, "you are a human devil?"

"Why are we playing at semantics?"

"I'm just trying to understand how you see yourself."

"I see myself as someone who is not to be trifled with."

"And you think I am trifling with you?"

"I think you are too smart for your own good," I said. "Your book of Ecclesiastes says not to be overly wise, lest you destroy yourself."

"You think I'm in danger of being overly wise?"

"You're in danger of something. Maybe inquisitiveness is more suitable a description."

"'Curiosity killed the cat'?"

"Precisely. 'Hang sorrow, care'll kill a cat, up-tails all, and a louse for the hangman.'"

"Shakespeare?"

"No, Ben Jonson. But Shakespeare said something similar around the same time. 'Though care killed a cat, thou hast mettle enough in thee to kill care.'"

"Would that I did have such mettle," Jael said.

"Do you not? You sit here in an abandoned house with a killer of thousands, and your heartrate is not even elevated."

The slightest smile tugged at the corner of her mouth. "I thought you didn't count."

"I don't. But it's at least thousands, as are my lovers."

She snorted. "You must have every disease under the sun."

"How very rude and unladylike a suggestion. But, no, as with injury, my undead body does not suffer such. You need not worry about catching a venereal disease from me, little Jael. Ah, but now, I think—yes—your heartrate is finally rising."

14

Jael turned her face away, but I saw the color bloom in her cheeks.

"Don't look at me like that," she said.

"And how am I looking at you, Jael?"

"Like you're a hungry dog, and I'm some treat to be devoured."

"I *am* hungry."

"You're making me uncomfortable."

"How cute. And how churlish of me—I really should be more professional about this kidnapping business."

"I thought you said you had not kidnapped me."

"Yes, well, perhaps we both enjoy semantics too much."

Jael pulled her jacket closer about her. She stared down at the oversized socks on her feet, and her brow furrowed in apparent concentration.

"What are you thinking?"

"Nothing," she said.

I chuckled. "What vast possibility lies within a woman's 'nothing.'"

"I guess you would know."

"Indeed, I would. You know, that quote about the cat earlier was from Shakespeare's play *Much Ado About Nothing*. I actually saw it performed under the man himself."

"I know."

I raised an eyebrow. "You knew I saw the play in Shakespeare's day?"

"No, I knew the cat quote was from that play. Or something like it. The similar quote by the other guy threw me off. But I was in a performance of the play in high school theater."

"Playing whom?"

Jael stared into the middle distance. "'He that hath a beard is more than a youth, and he that hath no beard is less than a man. He that is more than a youth is not for me, and he that is less than a man, I am not for him.'"

"Ah, Beatrice. A fine example of female fickleness."

"'Sigh no more, ladies, sigh no more, men were deceivers ever—one foot in sea and one on shore, to one thing constant never.'"

I smiled. "'Let me be that I am and seek not to alter me.'"

Jael met my gaze. "'Thou and I are too wise to woo peaceably.'"

"'I wish my horse had the speed of your tongue.' 'I love you with so much of my heart that none is left to protest.' 'I do love nothing in the world so well as you—is not that strange?'"

"'Would it not grieve a woman to be overmastered by a piece of valiant dust? To make an account of her life to a clod of wayward marl?'"

I uttered a mock gasp. "'What, my dear Lady Distain! Are you yet living?'"

"'Is it possible distain should die while she hath such meet food to feed it?'"

"'I do suffer love indeed, for I love thee against my will.'"

"'Well,'" Jael said, her tone airy, "'everyone can master a grief but he that has it.'"

"'Time goes on crutches till love have all his rites.'"

"'Foul words is but foul wind, and foul wind is but foul breath, and foul breath is noisome; therefore I will depart unkissed.'"

I dramatically clutched at my chest, as though stabbed. "Alas! 'Done to death by slanderous tongue.'"

We fell silent then, and I marveled that Jael had been able to match me in plucking fitting quotes from various parts and characters in the play to form a new dialogue. She must, indeed, have an eidetic memory.

Jael breathed a heavy sigh.

"What is it?"

"I just wish we could be having this conversation organically. We could be talking about religion and philosophy, quoting Solomon and Shakespeare, and otherwise getting to know each other over dinner. I invited you into my home, and you had to go and ruin everything. Now we're having this conversation under the terms of a hostage dynamic."

"Better to rip the bandage off quickly," I said. "We could have had some dates where I continued lying and wearing my masks, but dark truth is better than sunny fantasy. You can't tell me you would have gone on another date with me if you knew the truth about me."

"Is the forced presence of someone you claim to love really satisfying to you? Even if I, under compulsion, denied all that I held dear and became like you, would you really be happy, knowing you had ripped the one you love from all that she loved?"

"If you agreed to be with me forever, yes, I think I would be satisfied."

"You are wrong," Jael said.

"So, prove me wrong."

"I can't. I will never deny my Savior. No matter what you do to me."

"Time will tell. You will recant, eventually."

"'I cannot and will not recant anything, for to go against conscience is neither right nor safe. Here I stand, I can do no other.'"

"Don't quote Luther to me. I am more familiar with him than you could ever be. Do you have no thoughts or words of your own?"

"Some, I hope. But we stand on the shoulders of those who have gone before us."

"Another unoriginal sentiment."

"Well, admittedly, I am quite young. You said yourself that people don't often have much original thought or perspective until later in life."

"So, how can you stand by any belief or idea?"

"I believe I have some discernment," Jael said. "And why should a person have to build everything from scratch, when the end result would often appear identical to something that exists already?"

"If you lived for hundreds or thousands of years, you could thoroughly test every idea."

"As you have done?"

"I told you, I'm not much of a natural thinker. But *you* have a great mind to begin with. You could do so much if you would let me remake you into a new and better creature."

"I have a Maker already, and he has made me a new creation in Christ."

"I am not a nebulous spirit, Jael. I know what it is to be human, and I can truly help you in this life."

"The Son of God became a man, Jesus the Christ. He made himself lowly, emptied himself, and he knows our every pain and trial and temptation. You are no alternative at all."

"I was born around the same time as your Messiah."

"And before that, what were you? God was still God before the Incarnation. He is First and Last— 'I Am.' He has aseity, and you most certainly do not."

I chuckled. "Quite possibly, you are right, as I do not even know what aseity means. That's actually quite impressive, you know. A nineteen-year-old using a word I've never used in nineteen-hundred-plus years. Bravo, belletrist."

"It's not belletristic to use the word 'aseity'—it's economic."

"Your explanation of its economy defeats both purpose and claim."

A slight smile touched one corner of her mouth. "Touché."

"What, giving up so easily?"

"If I were to counter everything, you might accuse me of being pedantic or shrewish."

"'The lady doth protest too much, methinks.'"

"There you go with the accusation anyway."

"What," I said, "no Shakespearean rejoinder?"

"'More of your conversation would infect my brain.' 'You speak an infinite deal of nothing.'"

I smiled. "'Thine backward voice is to utter foul speeches and to detract.'"

"'I scorn you, scurvy companion.'"

"'I must tell you friendly in your ear, sell when you can, you are not for all markets.' 'You have such a February face, so full of frost, of storm, and cloudiness.'"

"'I'd beat thee,'" she said, "'but I would infect my hands.' 'Methink'st thou art a general offence and every man should beat thee.'"

"'Thy tongue outvenoms all the worms of the Nile.'"

"'I would thou wert clean enough to spit upon.'"

"'Virginity breeds mites,'" I said, "'much like cheese.'"

"'Out of my sight! Thou dost infect mine eyes.'"

"'You fustilarian! I'll tickle your catastrophe!'"

"'You poor, base, rascally, cheating, lack-linen mate!' 'Thou subtle, perjur'd, false, disloyal man!' 'The rankest compound of villainous smell that ever offended nostril.' 'Thou lump of foul deformity.' 'Thou are a boil, a plague sore.' 'Thou cream faced loon.' 'Thine face is not worth sunburning.' 'Would thou wouldst burst!'"

Whether she intended it or not, I heard a threat in the last half of her curation of quotes. The allusion to my pale skin, coupled with the idea of ultraviolet rays and disintegration.

Was her selection of insults merely coincidental, or did she truly think to kill me?

15

As I stood there, wondering if Jael was both innocent as a dove and shrewd as a serpent, she pushed off from the counter and crossed the kitchen to stand before me.

Haltingly, she reached up with one of her small hands, and she touched my cheek. Her skin was warm against my corpse-cold flesh.

"I'm sorry, Morcant. I got too carried away with my lines."

I was taken aback by her words, and her touch. By the seeming tenderness in her eyes.

An odd feeling nagged at me. I felt that, just maybe, I was not as in-control of the situation as I had believed.

I glanced out the window and saw that the dawn was not far off.

"You should get back to the cellar now," I said.

"Will you be there?"

She still stood before me, looking up with her large eyes, seeming like a child in the oversized jacket. And I felt a mix of conflicting emotions. Jael's enigmatic personality had me off my game and guard.

"No. No, I will sleep elsewhere."

"Please don't leave me alone."

"I thought that was exactly what you wanted me to do."

"Not alone in a cellar. If you will not let me go, at least stay with me."

"What happened to me being a clump of foul depravity?"

"A lump of foul deformity—though your depravity is plenty foul, as well."

"And you want me close?"

"'Keep your friends close and your enemies closer'?"

"And you think I can close my eyes in the same room as my declared enemy?"

"So don't close your eyes," she said. "Keep your eye on me if you don't trust me."

"I'll keep my eyes on you for reasons more than that."

She blushed, then turned and crossed the kitchen. At the entry to the cellar stairs, she glanced back, beckoned with her hand for me to follow, and descended the steps.

She's playing games with me, the vixen.

I nevertheless followed her down the steps, shutting the door behind me.

At the bottom of the stairs, I sat. Jael would not be getting past me to let light in—though I doubted any direct sunlight would reach down here, based on the position of the kitchen windows.

There was some wood in the cellar, but only in the form of shelves and steps.

In any case, I would keep my eye on her. I did not feel much like sleeping anyway.

The light from my torch had grown dim, so I retrieved some batteries from my bag and swapped out the old ones.

I set the torch back on its end, beam toward the ceiling, then returned to my place on the steps.

Jael strode to the opposite side of the cellar, then turned. She hugged herself against the chill of the underground room.

"Can I tell you about my childhood, Morcant?"

I shrugged. "Sure. I'm a killer therapist."

She did not laugh. She looked up at the ceiling for a moment, seeming to gather her thoughts.

16

"I was not supposed to live. My mother was a drug addict and mentally ill, and she tried to rip me apart with a wire hanger before I was born.

"My clothes hide a number of scars.

"It seems my mother passed out when she saw the blood coming from her.

"Her roommate found her then, and took her to the hospital, where I was delivered prematurely by cesarian.

"I was not supposed to live. The doctors didn't think I would make it through the night.

"But apparently I refused to die.

"I was given up for adoption. But no one wanted me. Perhaps the scars had something to do with it.

"Eventually, one of the nurses who took care of me had pity on me and convinced her husband that they should apply for adoption. They already had a daughter of their own, and had not intended to have any more.

"But, in the end, they adopted me.

"And I lived a fairly normal childhood for twelve years.

"When I was thirteen, I had my first drink. My parents thought I was at a simple sleepover, but boys and beers were added to the mix, and it got out of hand.

"I drank too much, and I don't remember how I got upstairs and in a room alone with a guy. But I remember we were making out, and he wanted to take things further.

"I started to lift my shirt, but as soon as he saw the scars on my belly, he recoiled.

"The next thing I remember is that I was alone and crying.

"Days later, while studying at a friend's house, I told her about what had happened. And I started crying again.

"My friend Liz comforted me. She held me, and she talked to me like I wished my older sister Kezia would. Liz and I were in the same grade, but she had been held back in school, and was about a year older than me.

"Sitting there on the bed in Liz's room, with her arm around me, I saw something surprising in her eyes. I had seen that look in the eyes of boys before they kissed me—but this was a girl.

"She leaned forward then, and she did kiss me. On the cheek at first, then, when I did not pull away, she kissed me on the lips.

"I was confused. At the time, I didn't have the words to explain even to myself what was happening. I knew of homosexuality as a concept, but not as a reality—not as a kid in such a small town.

ASHER ALLEN

"Liz told me not to tell anyone she had done that.

"I didn't tell. I was both terrified and thrilled by what I felt. I kept studying at Liz's house all through the school year, and we continued what she had started. We would make out all the time, mostly at her house, but sometimes in the locker room or somewhere else at school. It was always secret, but there was always the chance of getting caught—and that both frightened and excited me.

"As we matured, so did our relationship.

"We never did get caught, but after almost two years, I could keep the secret no longer. I came out to my mom.

"My adopted mother was not a Christian, but her family was Jewish, and she was quite traditional. She reacted very badly.

"I had never seen my mom act with any degree of violence toward anyone or anything—but that day, she slapped me hard. Twice.

138

"Then she started crying and wouldn't stop.

"When my dad got home from work, he wanted to know what was going on. Mom had promised not to tell when I'd said I had a secret to share, but then she went and told him everything.

"He didn't slap me or cry. He was just sad and disappointed.

"When Kezia inevitably found out, she was disgusted, and mocked me mercilessly.

"Obviously, I was grounded for the foreseeable future, but Liz snuck in through my window one night, after not hearing from me for a few days.

"When I told her what had happened, she slapped me too. For telling.

"She apologized immediately, but the damage was done.

"I stopped seeing her.

"But I did not turn away from my newfound interest in girls. I did not care what my parents thought.

"Well, I proceeded to cause a good deal of trouble at my school. But I won't get into that.

"That summer, my parents sent me to stay with my grandparents on my dad's side of the family. I knew they were religious, but I had always thought they were Jewish like my mom.

"But, no, they were Christians. When I found this out, I laughed and said they had not done a very good job with my dad, as he was very critical of Christianity.

"They made me go to church with them. And I hated it.

"At first, I didn't listen to the sermons at all. When I finally did, it was to seek out holes in the pastor's logic. Flaws in the Bible.

"I eventually became quite the student of the Scriptures in my pursuit of faults in the foundation.

"When at last I felt I had enough ammunition, I asked to speak with the pastor.

"He listened, not interrupting as I railed against religion at large and him personally. When I pointed out apparent contradictions or unjust laws in the Bible, he was able to answer some of the objections. Those he couldn't immediately answer, he wrote down, saying he would get back to me once he looked into the issue further.

"Well, most of the wind had left my sails, but I threw one last jab, saying that if he really believed his Scriptures, he should kill me, because I was a lesbian.

"He quoted Paul's first letter to the Corinthians, chapter six, where the apostle lists sinners of all sorts, including homosexuals, saying they will not inherit the kingdom of God. Then he read the following verse:

"'And such were some of you: but ye are washed, but ye are sanctified, but ye are justified in the name of the Lord Jesus, and by the Spirit of our God.'

"I didn't think that anything had changed that day. I didn't immediately turn from my ways or start enjoying church. But the words of the letter stuck with me. Before, I guess I had imagined I could never truly be a child of God even if I wanted to be. Some Christians had told me that a person guilty of homosexuality could never be counted among the redeemed. It was the unforgiveable sin.

"But Paul seemed to disagree. Seemed to suggest some of the early Christians had been homosexuals before conversion.

"Still, I didn't think it would work for me. Even if I believed Jesus was real, that he was the Son of God and had done the things the Bible said—well, I still had these desires that were condemned. Maybe those early Christians had 'prayed the gay away,' but I had no hope of that.

"I finally brought this up with the pastor, and I still remember his words.

"'All Christians struggle with temptations. All wrestle with intrusive thoughts and dark desires. Particular strongholds of sin will, with God's help, weaken over time. But just as another woman may struggle with lust toward a man, you may struggle with lust toward a woman. Both of you can resist temptation with the Spirit's strength as you grow in Christ.'

"It was still summer, and I was still with my grandparents, still wrestling with all of this—when my mom died.

"My parents had been on their way to see me. My mom was driving, and she swerved off the road to avoid a deer. She crashed into a tree, and a branch impaled her. My dad, in the passenger seat, was paralyzed from the waist down.

"Many children try to find ways to blame themselves for the death of a parent, and I was no different. If only I had not been away . . . if only they had not been coming to see me . . . if only, if only.

"This sense of guilt, real or imagined, only added to the shame I was already feeling over my lifestyle.

"I suppose it was just as likely—or more likely—that the tragedy of my mom's death would have driven me further away from God. But it didn't. I wanted all the more to know the truth about life and death, why evil existed, where I fit in the grand story of everything.

"I am not certain when I truly believed and trusted Christ. I only know that at some point in my fifteenth year, I could no longer deny that I longed for his Spirit, and wept to consider I might be a child of God.

"I was baptized at my grandparents' church, and my life has never been the same.

"I still struggle with sinful thoughts and desires sometimes. But not like I used to. And I know peace now, as I never did before.

"I believe that someday, I will marry a man. I believe I will find delight in him and in his body. And I will bear our children.

"Or perhaps not. Maybe I will never be attracted to a man, and will remain single. But, in any case, I do not claim to be a lesbian or bisexual. I am just a sinner, saved by grace alone, by faith in Christ alone, to the glory of God alone."

17

Jael fell silent, and I guessed that was the end of her story.

"Why did you tell me all that? Do you think to convince me to become a Christian by telling me your grandparents forced you to go to church at an impressionable age, and you blamed yourself for your mother's death?"

Jael smiled sadly. "No, Morcant. I told you my story so you would know something about me. I am Jael. A real person, with a real history, real scars, struggles, desires, insecurities, dreams. I just want you to know that as you decide what you will do with me, or to me."

I had no ready response, and Jael walked to the side of the room. She knelt before the spacious shelves and, like a sleepy child, crawled onto the lowest one. She curled up there on the makeshift bed, her back toward me, and shifted about some as though trying to get comfortable enough to sleep.

And I felt something like shame.

I knew I was just tired. And hungry. Infatuated, perhaps.

But the girl plucked at the cadaverous cords of my black heart.

No. No, I must not allow this.

I rose and paced the room.

I would have my way, and Jael would come to love me. She would forget about her past life and her dreams.

Why must I be drawn to one such as you, Jael? A Christian. *A born-again, die-hard, sold-out Way-follower.*

You make me sick. Your obsession with a Jewish carpenter called Yeshua makes me ill.

And you make me sick with love. Or is it just obsession?

I am jealous for you, little Jael.

I heard a snap, like a board breaking, and looked over to where Jael lay.

She was motionless. With her back toward me, I could not tell whether or not she was asleep.

She was beautiful. She did not possess the voluptuousness, luxuriant trappings, or goddess-like appearance of the women I had often chosen for myself. Yet, somehow, her ordinary sort of loveliness touched a deeper type of desire in me.

Was it actually her spirit that was beautiful?

Did that even make sense? Was not beauty—in my book, at least—aesthetic perfection? Design of optimal ocular titillation?

This girl was a thorn in my side. She would ruin me if I let her.

I stopped pacing.

I must not let her. I must be strong. Logical.

"My will be done." I looked to where Jael lay. "You hear me, Jael? *My* will be done."

She did not stir.

"I know you are awake. And I'm done with your games, you little slave of God."

Still, she lay motionless and quiet.

"I know you hear me. If you do not give up your God and follow me, I will paint this town red! And I mean that very literally. I will hang your father with his own guts, and he will think that a mercy after he watches what I do to his eldest daughter."

Still, Jael did not move from her place. But I saw her tremble.

I sprang to her side, seized her by the jacket, and dragged her off her shelf-bed.

She kept her eyes and mouth shut, tucked her arms and legs as she curled into a fetal position.

She seemed so much like a child in that moment. A child being abused.

And I lost all heart to harm her.

I released my hold on her jacket and stepped back.

And I realized she was right. I was a monster.

I had always accepted this fact to some degree, but now, for the first time, it brought me shame that smote me to my rotten core.

Turning my face away from Jael, I swore under my breath, cursing the day I met this girl.

To preserve my sanity, I must get away from her. But I could not.

I was more her captive than she was mine.

Then I saw the shelf on which Jael had been lying.

At the back edge of the plank, a jagged section of wood was missing.

Of course, old planks sometimes break away in shard-like lengths like that, but I was certain the board had been intact when I first entered the room. I always look for those sorts of things, as it is a matter of life and death for me.

Then I realized. That was why Jael had lain there in the first place, and why her back had been toward me. She had seen the crack in the plank.

That was the cause of the snap I had heard. Jael arming herself.

She knew, or suspected, the means of my death.

Strangely, I felt no rage.

Only sadness.

Why? Why you?

Why, Jael?

I turned from the shelf, walked past the spot where Jael still lay curled up, and over to my bugout bag.

I sat down, took out my journal, and I wrote the events of the past night and day. Processing my thoughts. I wrote for hours, barely even utilizing my inhuman speed.

And Jael lay there on the floor, still and silent as a corpse.

18

This may be the final entry in my journal.

I know Jael has a makeshift stake.

And I will not take it from her.

She must either love me or end me.

If we speak again, I will tell her she can leave. But I hope she stays.

Beauty may yet love the Beast.

In a very real sense, Jael holds my heart in her hands.

I will lie down and sleep now, and pray the angel may have pity upon this devil.

But if not, it is for the best. I want to love her, but my obsession is only hurting her.

Save me, Jael. Or deliver me from this body of death.

Jael

When I was certain the monster Morcant was sleeping, I slipped the long shard of wood from my sleeve.

With painfully slow movements, I crept toward my captor.

When, at last, I knelt beside him, he looked almost peaceful in his repose. Part of me wanted to kiss his pale forehead, tuck a blanket close, and wish sweet dreams upon him. Or lie down beside him, rest my head upon his chest, feel his strong arms embrace me.

I exhaled a quivering sigh.

Whispers of Stockholm Syndrome. Nothing more.

I placed the splinter-sharp tip of the stake over his heart.

My hands began to shake, and I realized I would not follow through if I allowed myself to delay.

I drove the stake home, putting my entire weight behind the blow. And I gave vent to a wrenching cry of rage and regret.

Morcant's eyelids flew open. His jaw stretched wide, but no sound escaped. He fixed his gaze upon me, but I saw no anger or even shock. And no fight.

For an interminable moment, he just stared at me with an expression I almost mistook for affection. Or gratitude.

Then, as if all the blood in his body had turned to acid, his flesh sizzled and popped. In seconds, his clothes, skin, muscles, and organs were gone. A blackened skeleton remained for a moment, then crumbled to a pile of ash.

I dropped the stake and fell backward.

What had I done?

He had trusted me. He might have begun to turn from his wicked ways.

And now I had destroyed him.

I am so sorry, Morcant. Sorry you had to die in my time. How I wish you had died as a man millennia ago.

My own heart still pounding, I crawled forward, staring at the cooling heap of char-dust.

"'Dust thou art, and unto dust shalt thou return.'"

Tears came then, and fell upon the immolated remains of a monster that had once been a man.

About the Author

Asher Allen is a lifelong teller of stories, both the fanciful and the factual. He studied journalism at the Defense Information School, and traveled the world chronicling true accounts during his time as a military journalist. Now a dedicated fictionist, he writes in a variety of genres, with a focus on the fantastical.